CREATED BY
Pendleton Ward

WRITTEN
Ryan N

ILLUSTRATED BY
Shelli Paroline and Braden Lamb

ADDITIONAL COLORS BY
Lisa Moore

"ADVENTURE TIM"

ILLUSTRATED BY
Mike Holmes

COLORS BY STUDIO PARLAPÀ

LETTERS BY
Steve Wands

COVER BY
Chris Houghton

COLORS BY KASSANDRA HELLER

EDITOR
Shannon Watters

ASSISTANT EDITOR
Adam Staffaroni

TRADE DESIGN
Stephanie Gonzaga

With special thanks to
Marisa Marionakis, Rick Blanco, Curtis Lelash, Laurie Halal-Ono, Keith
Mack, Kelly Crews and the wonderful folks at Cartoon Network.

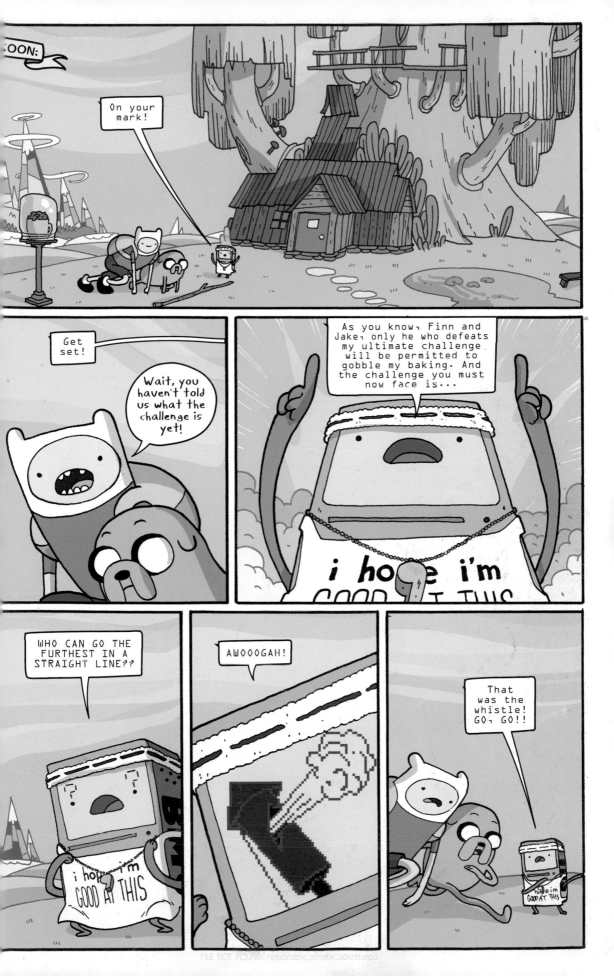

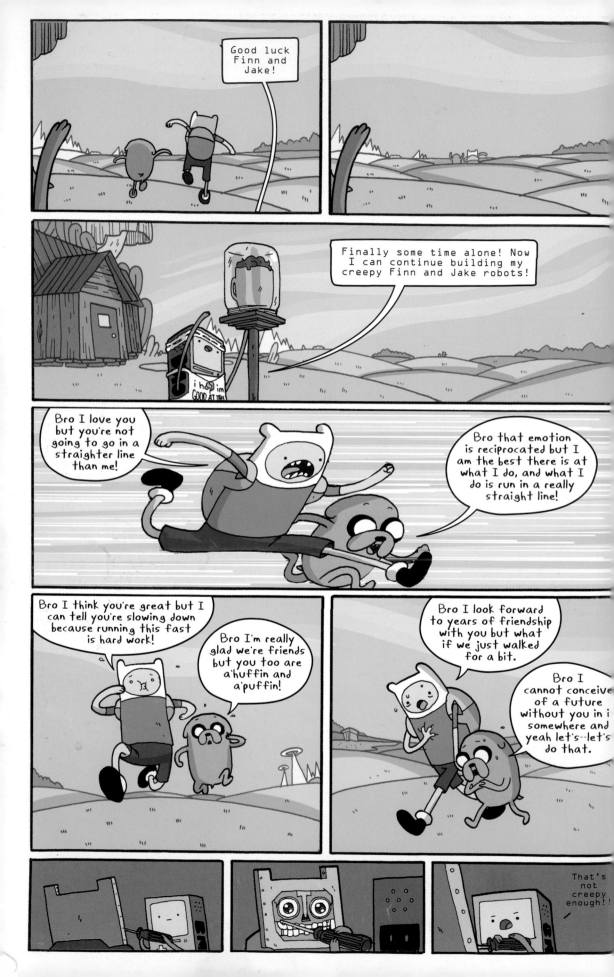

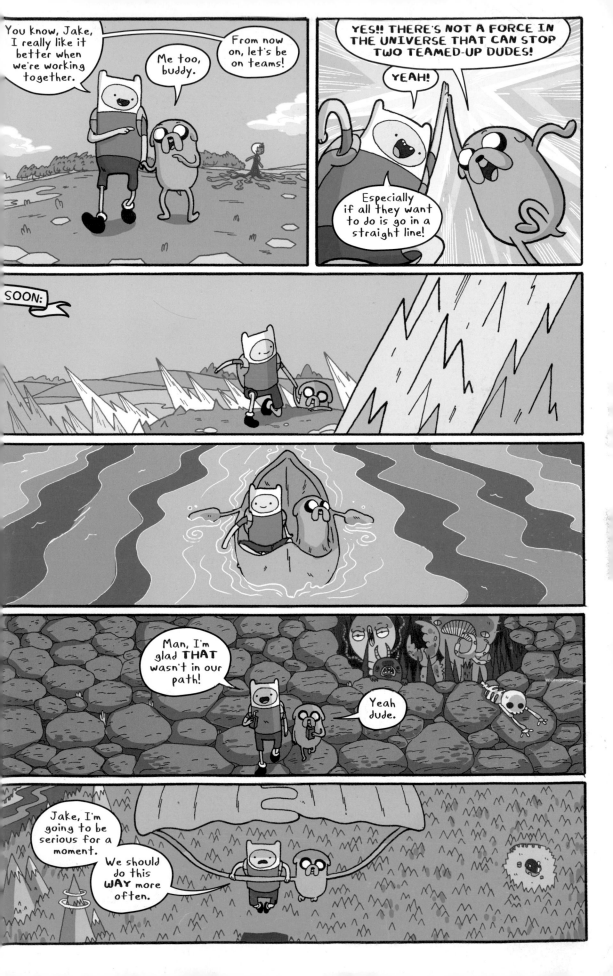

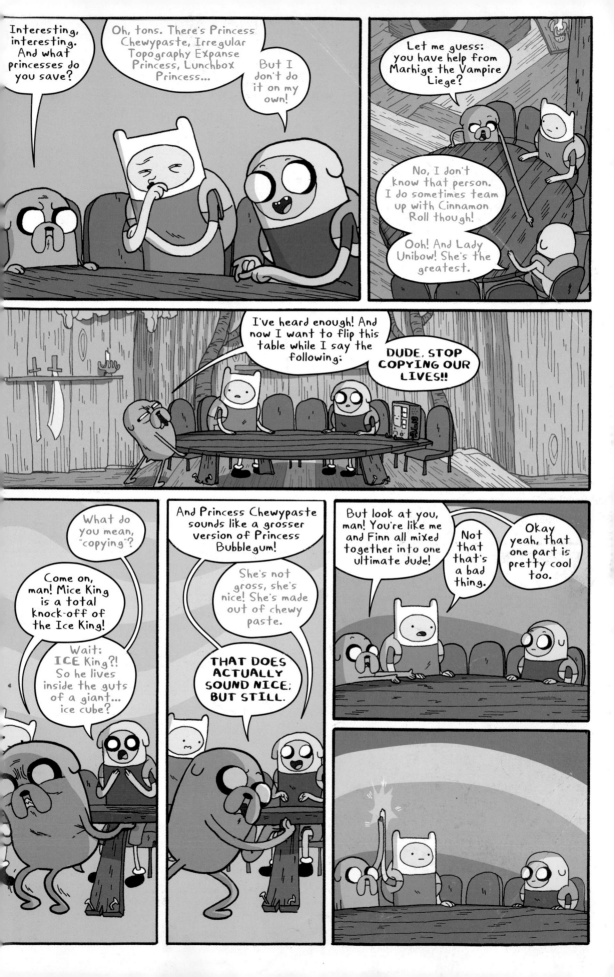

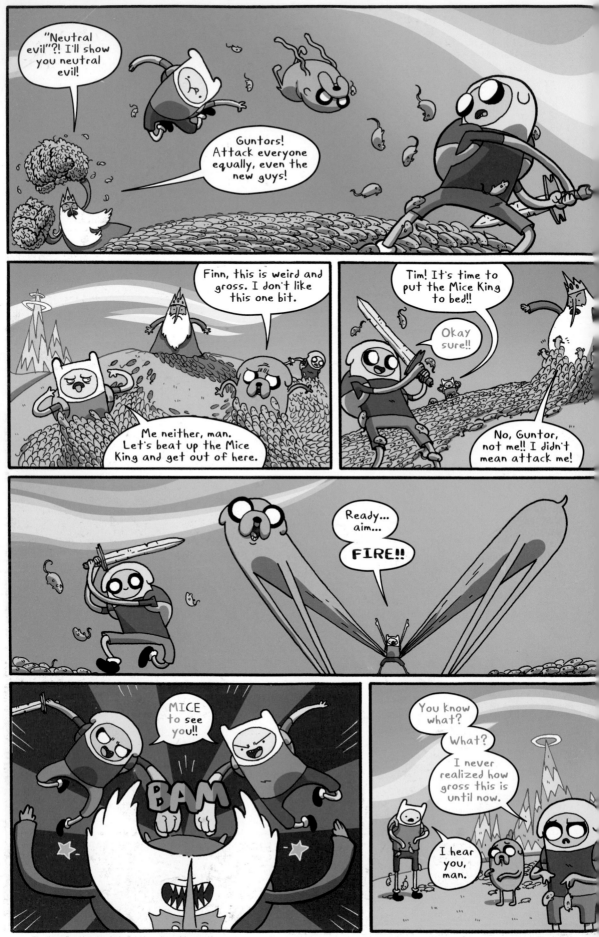

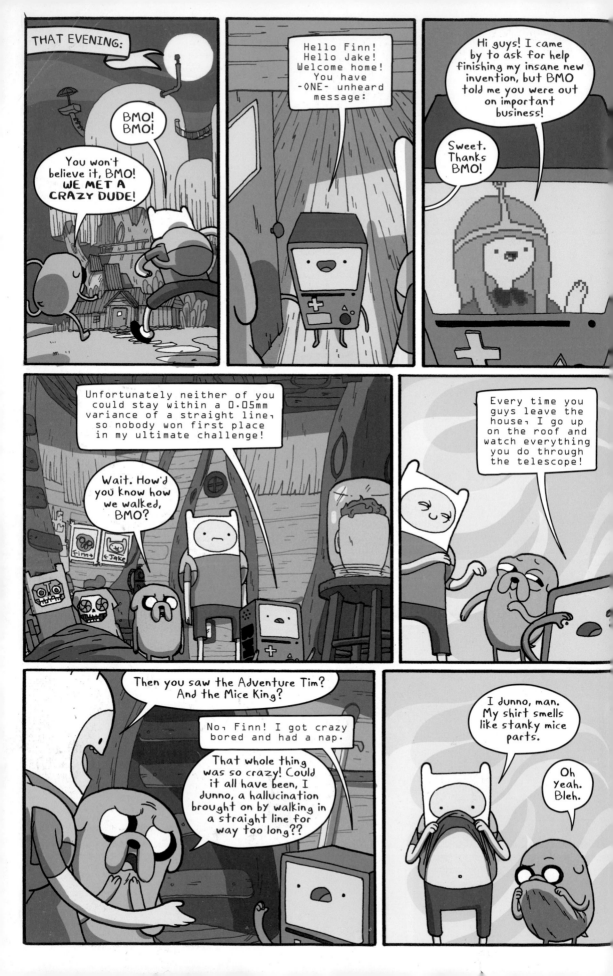

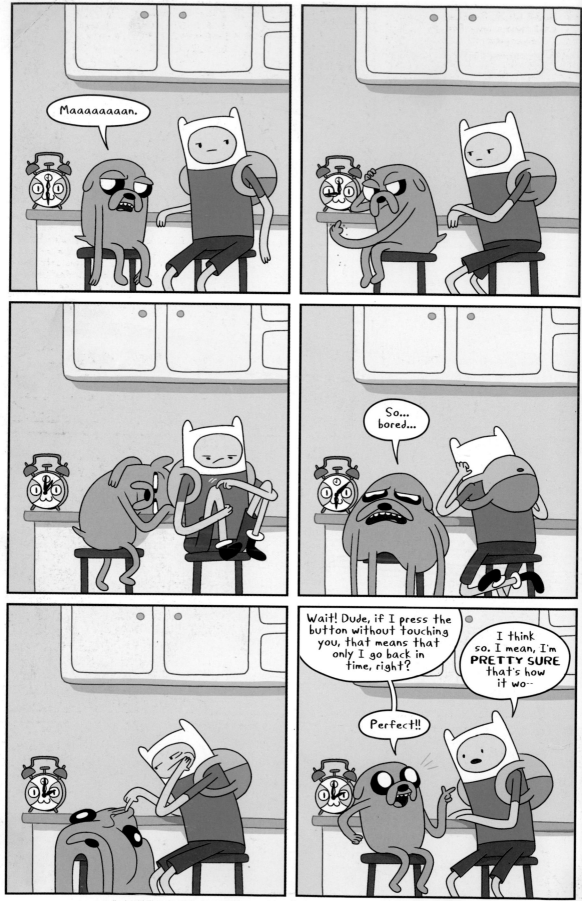

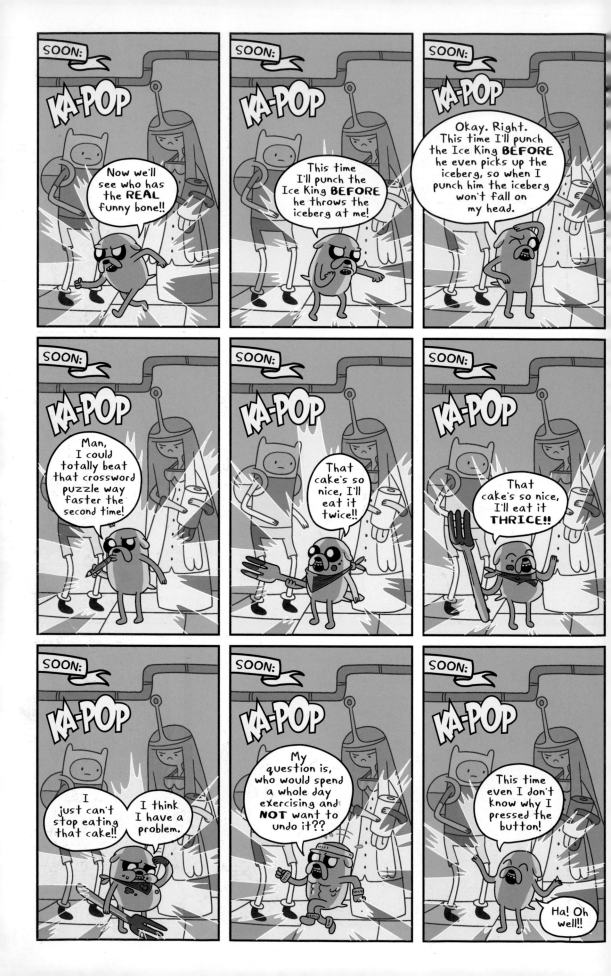

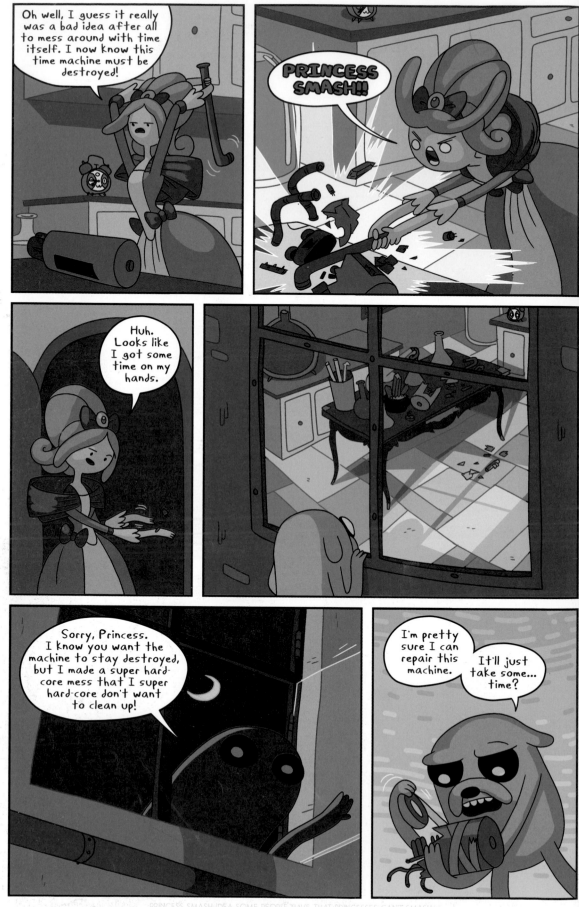

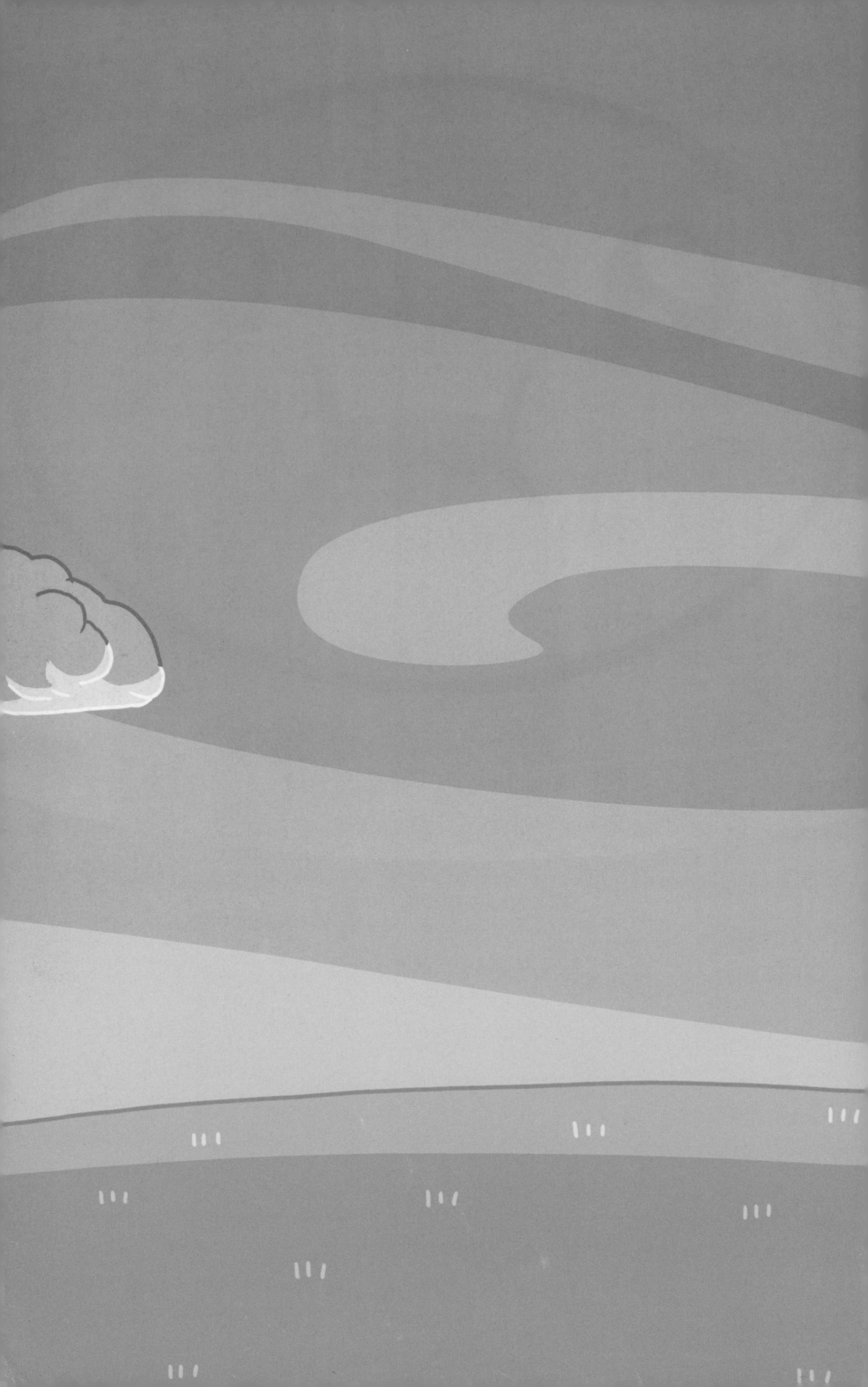

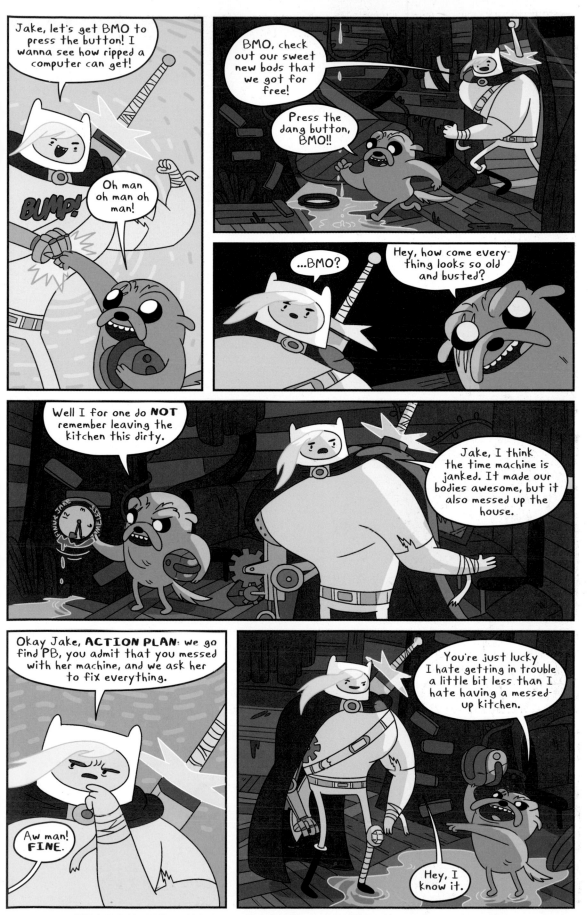

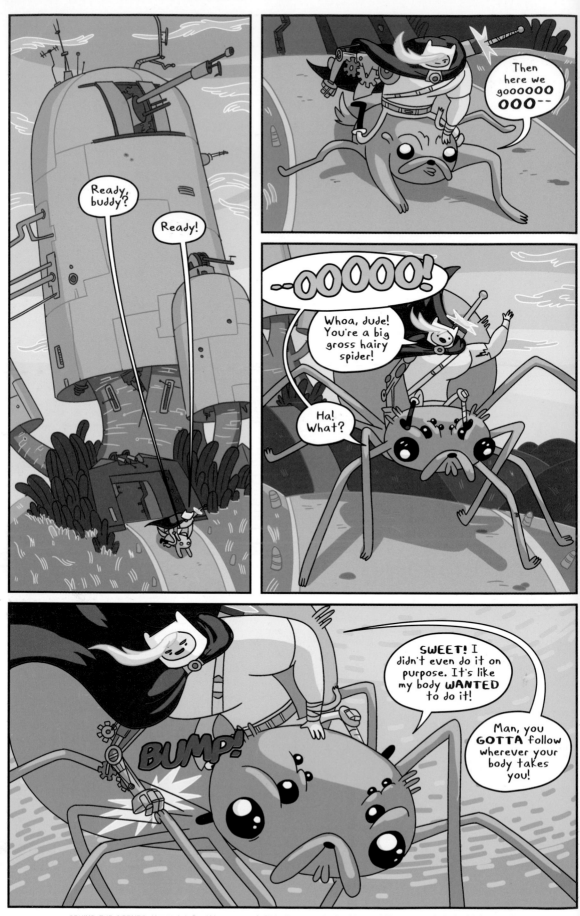

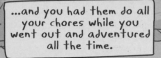

...and you had them do all your chores while you went out and adventured all the time.

But we didn't realize their fatal flaw! There was a bug in their programming or something, because as soon as they got wet, these robots turned HECKUVA EVIL.

The robots renamed themselves from "F1NN" and "J4KE" to "TERM N8R" and "KILL-O-TRON". At first we thought it was cute! Then they started trying to terminate us!!

You barely made it out alive.

We duplicated their lazers. We upgraded ourselves. I got my Science Hand, Finn got a neato arm and Jake started changing into more powerful forms. We can destroy individual robots more easily now, but they're still a huge threat in numbers. We must remain...vigilant.

NEPTR still helps us fight, but even in the future pies are still pretty useless against robots. And BMO? Well, nobody's seen BMO since the robots first returned that morning fifteen years ago.

ACTUAL WRITING TIP: to write a character talking with something in their mouth, just put your own fist in your mouth and write down the sounds you make. I--kinda like writing alone.

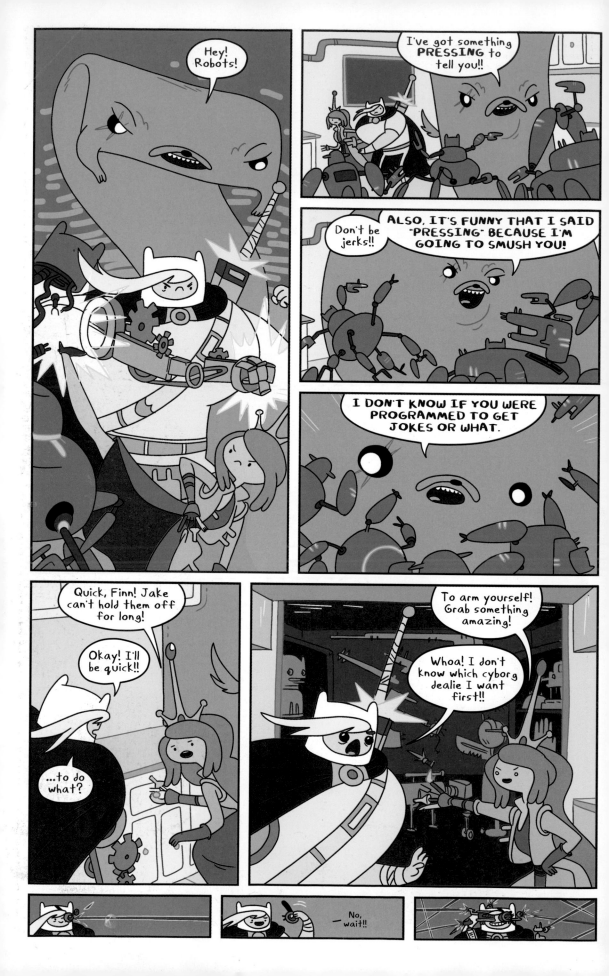

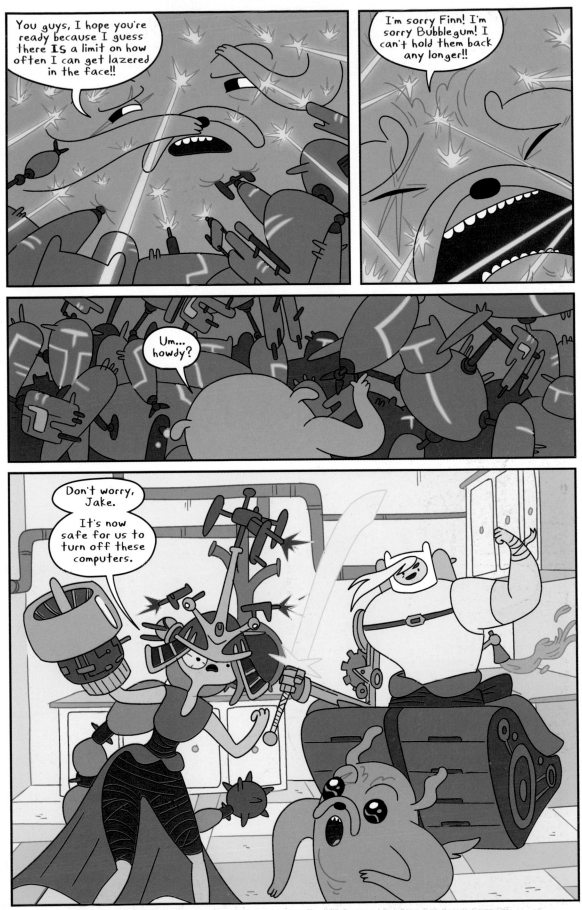

If you looked at my search history you would find "Jake in a fedora," "does Jake look cool in a fedora," "I want to see Jake in a fedora" and "what if Jake had extra arms and a fedora, is that illegal??"

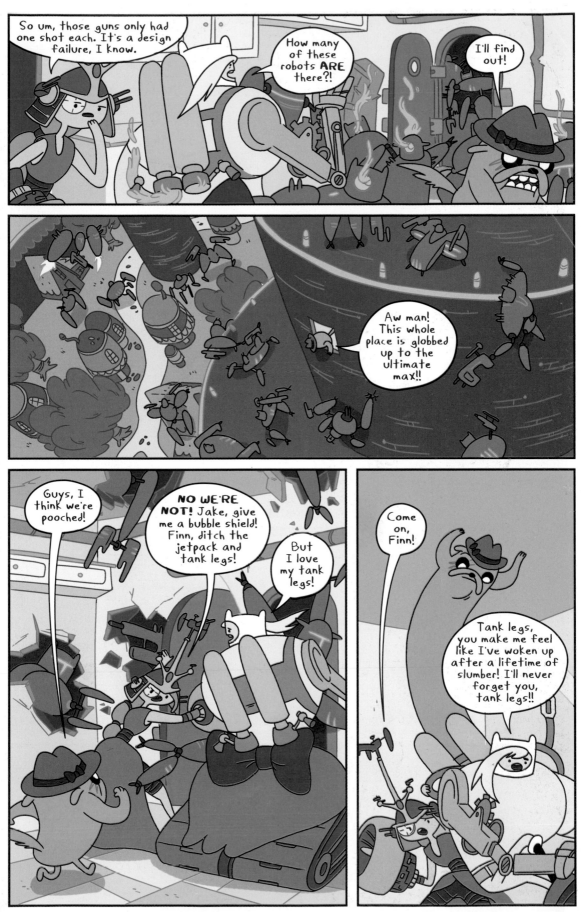

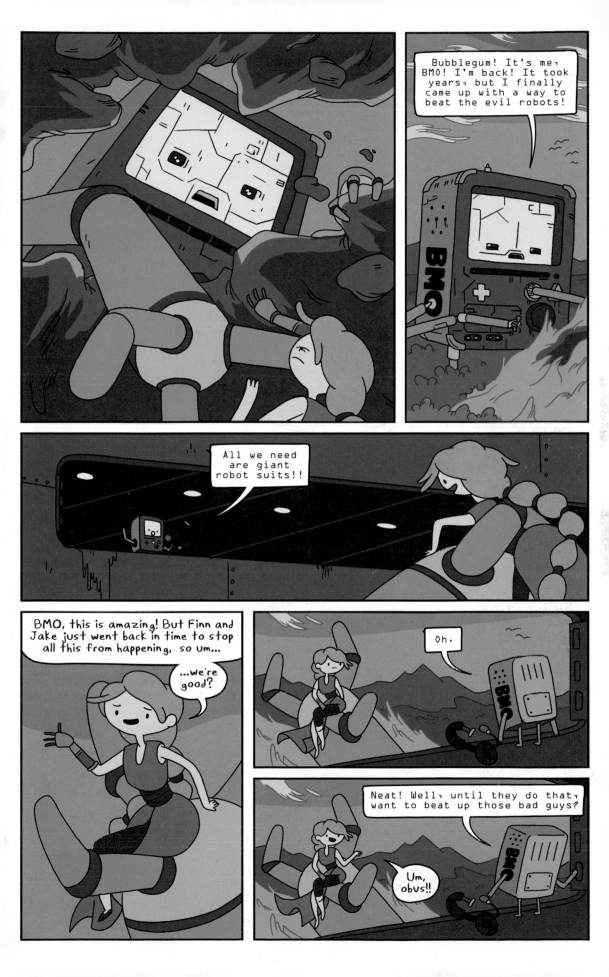

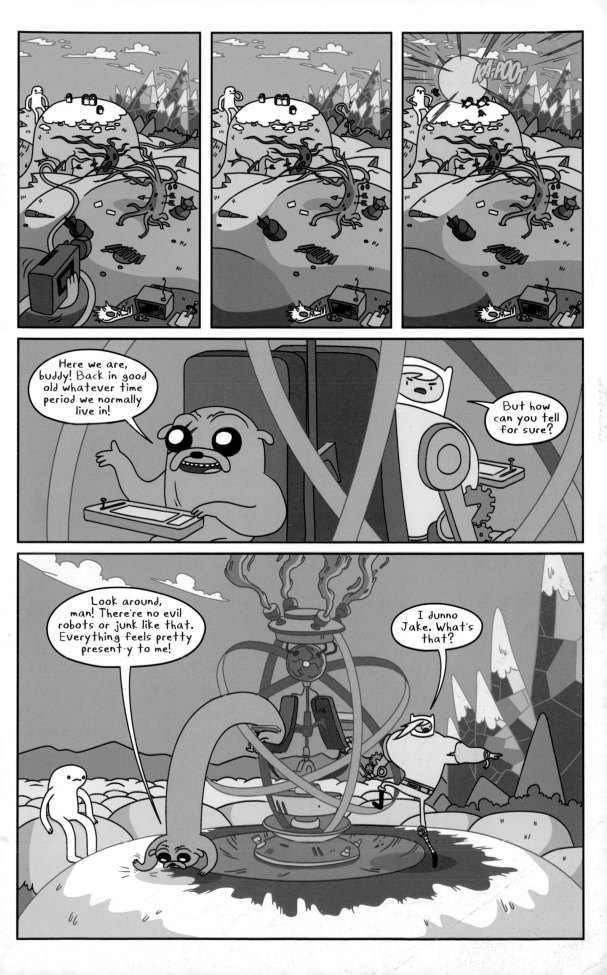

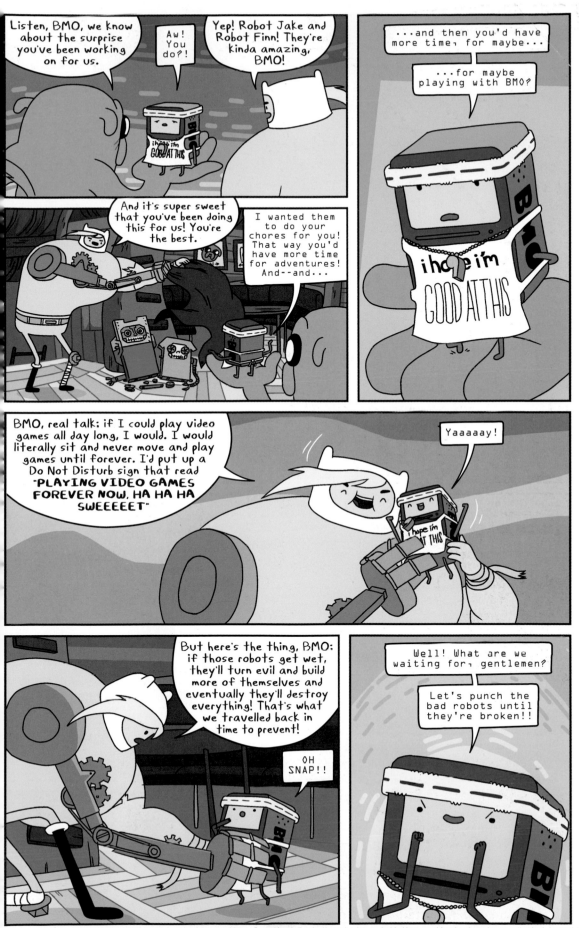

Listen, BMO, we know about the surprise you've been working on for us.

Aw! You do?!

Yep! Robot Jake and Robot Finn! They're kinda amazing, BMO!

...and then you'd have more time, for maybe...

...for maybe playing with BMO?

And it's super sweet that you've been doing this for us! You're the best.

I wanted them to do your chores for you! That way you'd have more time for adventures! And--and...

i hope i'm GOOD AT THIS

BMO, real talk: if I could play video games all day long, I would. I would literally sit and never move and play games until forever. I'd put up a Do Not Disturb sign that read "PLAYING VIDEO GAMES FOREVER NOW, HA HA HA SWEEEEET"

Yaaaaay!

But here's the thing, BMO: if those robots get wet, they'll turn evil and build more of themselves and eventually they'll destroy everything! That's what we travelled back in time to prevent!

OH SNAP!!

Well! What are we waiting for, gentlemen?

Let's punch the bad robots until they're broken!!

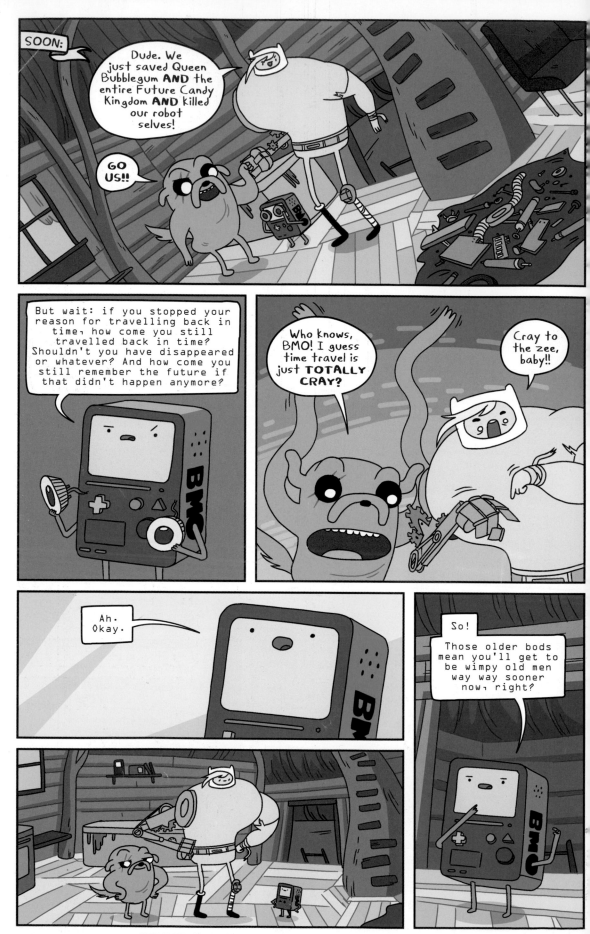

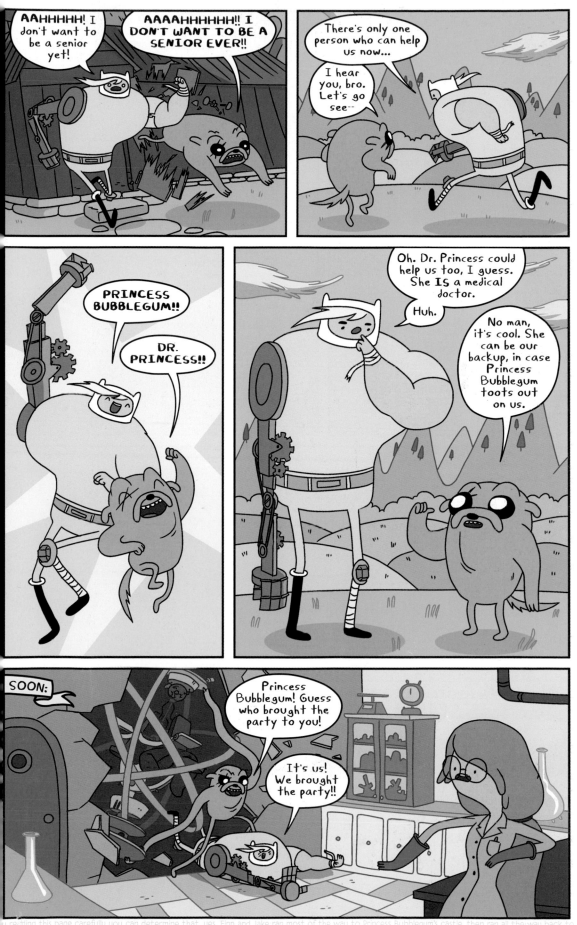

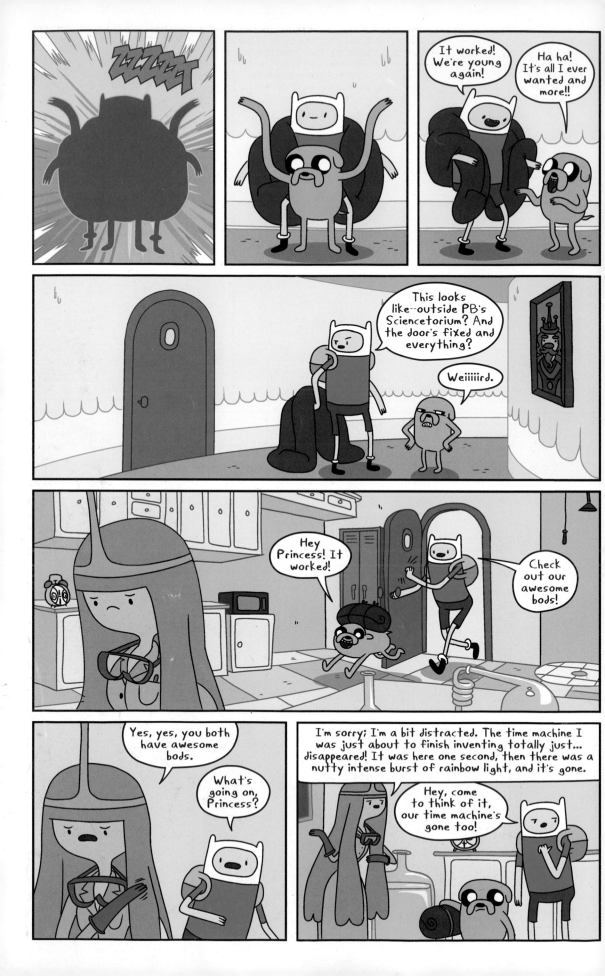

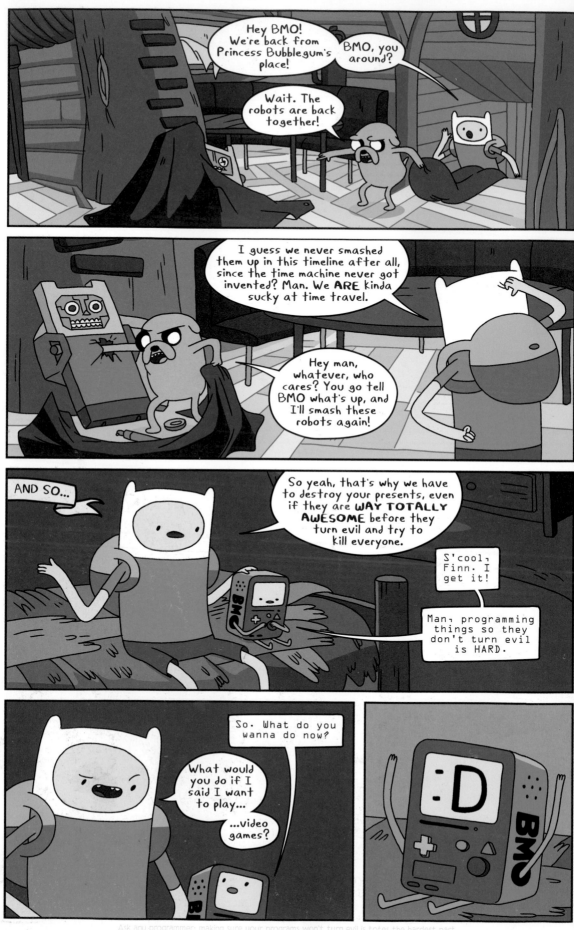

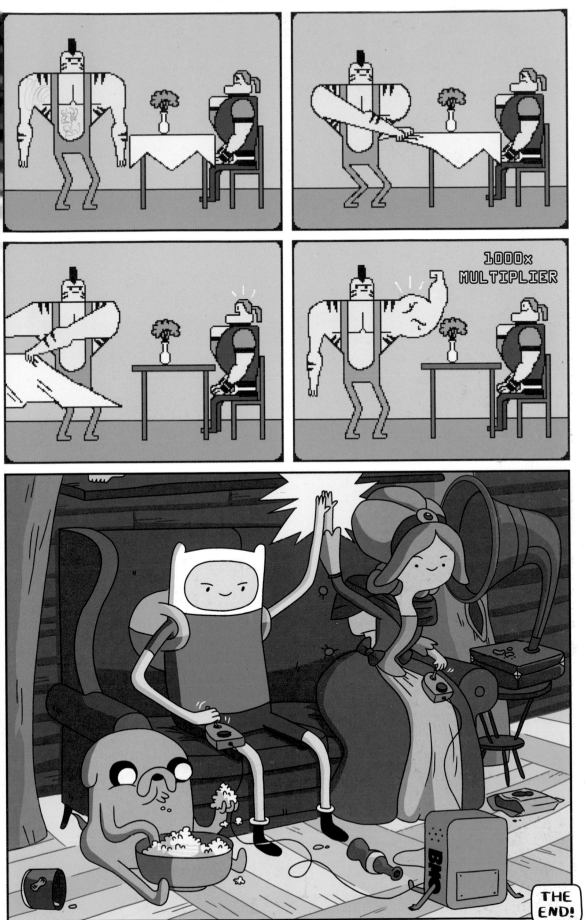

1000x MULTIPLIER

THE END!

COVER GALLERY

CHRIS
HOUGHTON

Cover 7C:
Graham Annable

-GRAHAM-

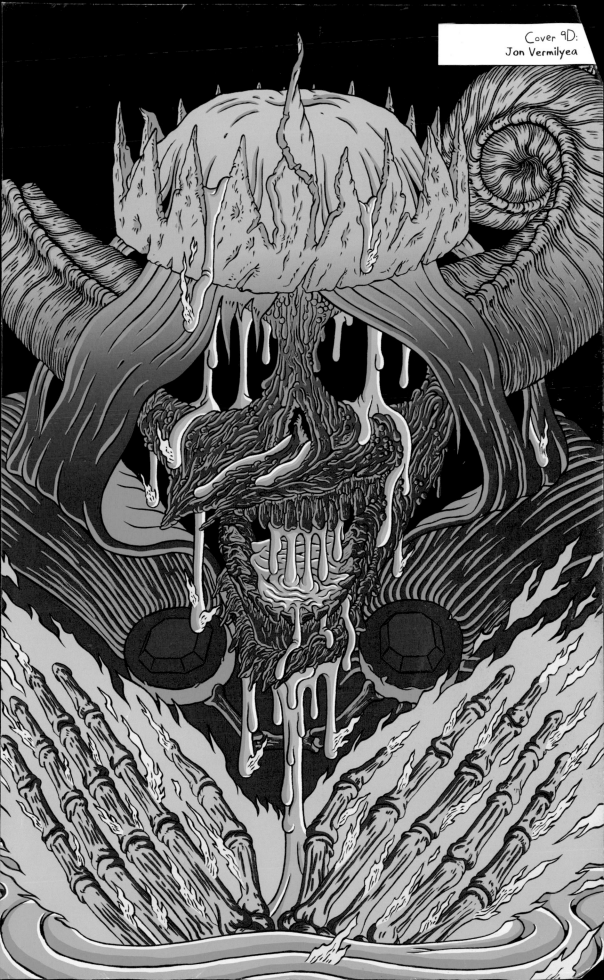